For Patrycja

Scholastic Canada Ltd.
604 King Street West, Toronto, Ontario M5V 1E1, Canada

Scholastic Inc.
557 Broadway, New York, NY 10012, USA

Scholastic Australia Pty Limited
PO Box 579, Gosford, NSW 2250, Australia

Scholastic New Zealand Limited
Private Bag 94407, Botany, Manukau 2163, New Zealand

Scholastic Children's Books
Euston House, 24 Eversholt Street, London NW1 1DB, UK

www.scholastic.ca

The artwork in this book is acrylic (with pens and pencils) on watercolour paper.

Library and Archives Canada Cataloguing in Publication
Blabey, Aaron, author, illustrator
        I need a hug / Aaron Blabey.

ISBN 978-1-4431-4889-4 (hardback).--ISBN 978-1-4431-4896-2 (paperback)

        I. Title.

PZ10.3.B519In 2016   j823'.92   C2016-900379-5

First published by Scholastic Australia in 2015.
This edition published by Scholastic Canada Ltd. in 2016.

6 5 4 3 2 1   Printed in Malaysia 108   16 17 18 19 20

Aaron Blabey

I Need a Hug

Scholastic Canada Ltd.
Toronto New York London Auckland Sydney
Mexico City New Delhi Hong Kong Buenos Aires